MR. SMALL

by Roger Hargreaves

EGMONT

Mr Small was very small. Probably the smallest person you've ever seen in your whole life.

Or perhaps the smallest person you've never seen in your whole life, because he was so small you probably wouldn't see him anyway.

Mr Small was about as big as a pin, which isn't very big at all, so perhaps we should say that Mr Small was as small as a pin!

Mr Small lived in a small house underneath a daisy at the bottom of Mr Robinson's garden.

It was a very nice house, although very tiny, and it suited Mr Small very well indeed. He liked living there.

Now, this story is all about the time Mr Small decided to get a job.

The trouble was, what sort of job could Mr Small do? After all, there aren't that many small jobs!

Mr Small had thought about it for a long time, but hadn't had any ideas.

Not one!

He was thinking about it now, while he was having lunch.

He was having half a pea, one crumb, and a drop of lemonade.

Mr Small thought and thought while he was eating his big lunch, but it was no use.

Thinking just made him thirsty, so he had another drop of lemonade.

"I know," he thought to himself, "after lunch I'll go and see Mr Robinson and ask his advice."

So after lunch he left his house and walked to Mr Robinson's house at the top of the garden.

It was quite a long walk for somebody as small as Mr Small, and halfway there he stopped for a rest.

He sat on a pebble, feeling quite out of breath.

A worm crawled by, and stopped.

"Good afternoon, Mr Small," said the worm.

"Good afternoon, Walter," said Mr Small to the worm, whom he knew quite well.

"Out for a walk, are you?" asked Walter.

"Going to see Mr Robinson," replied Mr Small.

"Oh!" said Walter.

"About a job," added Mr Small.

"Oh!" said Walter the worm again, and crawled off.

Walter was a worm of very few words.

After he'd rested for a while, Mr Small set off again and walked all the rest of the way to Mr Robinson's house without stopping once.

When he got there, he climbed up the steps to Mr Robinson's door.

He knocked at the door.

Nobody heard him!

He knocked again at the door.

Nobody heard him!

The trouble was, you see, that if you're as small as Mr Small, you don't have a very loud knock.

Mr Small looked up.

There, high above his head, was a doorbell.

"How can I ring the bell when I can't reach it?" thought Mr Small to himself.

He started to climb up the wall, brick by brick, to reach the bell.

He had climbed up four bricks when he made the mistake of looking down.

"Oh dear," he said, and fell.

BANG!!

"Ouch!" said Mr Small, rubbing his head.

Just then Mr Small heard footsteps.

It was the postman.

The postman came to the door, posted his letters, and was just about to leave when he heard a voice.

"Hello," said the voice.

The postman looked down.

"Hello," he said to Mr Small. "Who are you?"

"I'm Mr Small," said Mr Small. "Will you ring the bell for me, please?"

"Of course I will," replied the postman in answer to Mr Small's question and, reaching out, he pressed the bell with his finger.

"Thank you," said Mr Small.

"My pleasure," said the postman, and off he went.

Mr Small heard footsteps coming to the door.

The door opened.

Mr Robinson opened the door and looked out.

"That's funny," he said. "I'm sure I heard somebody ring the bell!"

He was about to shut the door when he heard a little voice.

"Hello," said the voice. "Hello, Mr Robinson."

Mr Robinson looked down, and down.

"Hello," he said. "What are you doing here?"

"I've come to ask your advice," said Mr Small to Mr Robinson.

"Well," said Mr Robinson. "You'd better come in and have a talk."

Mr Small followed Mr Robinson into the house, and, perched on the arm of Mr Robinson's favourite chair, he told him how he couldn't think of a job that he could do.

Mr Robinson sipped a cup of tea, and listened.

"So you see," Mr Small explained, "how difficult it is."

"Yes, I can see that," said Mr Robinson. "But leave it to me!"

Mr Robinson knew a lot of people.

Mr Robinson knew somebody who worked in a restaurant, and arranged for Mr Small to work there.

Putting mustard into mustard pots!

But Mr Small kept falling into the pots and getting covered in mustard, so he left that job.

Mr Robinson knew somebody who worked in a sweetshop, and arranged for Mr Small to work there.

Serving sweets!

But Mr Small kept falling into the sweet jars, so he left that job.

Mr Robinson knew somebody who worked in a place where they made matches, and arranged for Mr Small to work there.

Packing matches into boxes!

But Mr Small kept getting shut in the boxes with the matches, so he left that job.

Mr Robinson knew somebody who worked on a farm, and arranged for Mr Small to work there.

Sorting out the brown eggs from the white eggs!

But Mr Small kept getting trapped by the eggs, so he left that job.

"What are we going to do with you?" Mr Robinson asked Mr Small one evening.

"Don't know!" said Mr Small in a small voice.

"I've got one more idea," said Mr Robinson. "I know somebody who writes children's books. Perhaps you could work for him."

So, the following day, Mr Robinson took Mr Small to meet the man who wrote children's books.

"Can I work for you?" Mr Small asked the man.

"Yes, you can," replied the man. "Pass me that pencil and tell me all about the jobs you've been doing. Then I'll write a book about it. I'll call it *Mr Small*," he added.

"But children won't want to read a book all about me!" exclaimed Mr Small.

"Yes, they will," replied the man. "They'll like it very much!"

And you did.

Didn't you?